TINY

To   all
the kitties out there
who need a home,
and to everyone
who has ever
opened their
heart to
o n e
♡

Balzer + Bray is an imprint of HarperCollins Publishers.

Tiny Kitty, Big City
Copyright © 2021 by Tim Miller
All rights reserved. Manufactured in China.

www.harpercollinschildrens.com

ISBN 978-0-06-241442-7

This book was made with acrylic gouache, with digital touch-ups. Also my cat was sitting in my lap while I worked,
so you might find some of her hair in the pictures.
Typography by Dana Fritts
21 22 23 24 25 SCP 10 9 8 7 6 5 4 3 2 1

❖
First Edition

KITTY, BIG CITY

by Tim Miller

BALZER + BRAY
An Imprint of HarperCollins*Publishers*

Tiny kitty.

Crowded city.

Speedy kitty.

Noisy city.

Hiding kitty.

Scary city.

Brave kitty.

Sunshine city.

Lazy kitty.

Lunchtime city.

Hungry kitty.

Playful kitty.

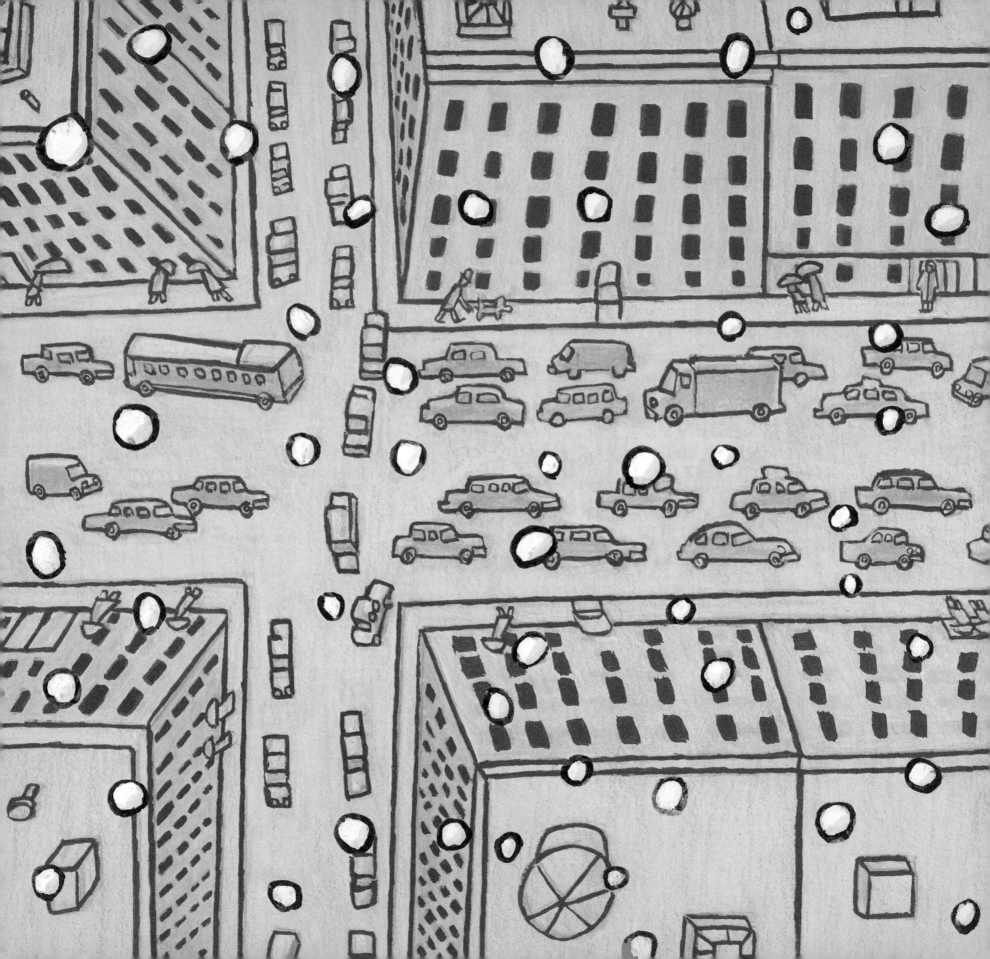

Snowy city.

Cold kitty.

Nighttime city.

Curious kitty.

Swinging city.

Singing kitty.

Bravo city.

Purring kitty.

Loving city.

Loving kitty.

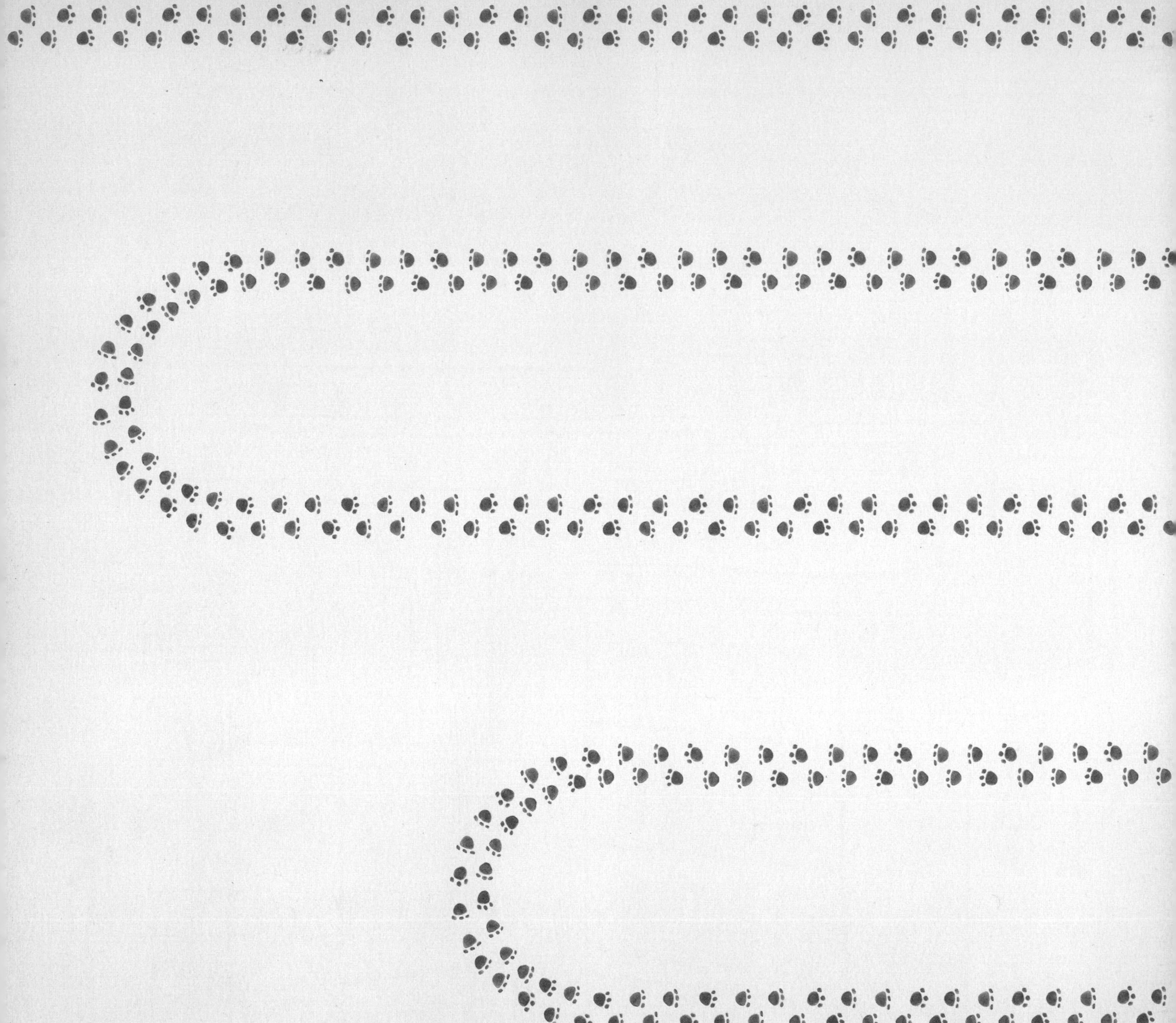